I0682349

Old-World Japan

Also from Westphalia Press

westphaliapress.org

The Idea of the Digital University

Bulwarks Against Poverty in America

Treasures of London

Avate Garde Politician

L'Enfant and the Freemasons

Baronial Bedrooms

Making Trouble for Muslims

Philippine Masonic Directory ~ 1918

Paddle Your Own Canoe

Opportunity and Horatio Alger

Careers in the Face of Challenge

Bookplates of the Kings

The Boy Chums Cruising in Florida Waters

Freemasonry in Old Buffalo

Original Cables from the Pearl Harbor Attack

Social Satire and the Modern Novel

The Essence of Harvard

The Genius of Freemasonry

A Definitive Commentary on Bookplates

James Martineau and Rebuilding Theology

No Bird Lacks Feathers

Gems of Song for the Eastern Star

Crime 3.0

Anti-Masonry and the Murder of Morgan

Understanding Art

Spies I Knew

Lodge "Himalayan Brotherhood" No. 459 C.E.

Ancient Masonic Mysteries

Collecting Old Books

Masonic Secret Signs and Passwords

Death Valley in '49

Lariats and Lassos

Mr. Garfield of Ohio

The Wisdom of Thomas Starr King

The French Foreign Legion

War in Syria

Naturism Comes to the United States

New Sources on Women and Freemasonry

Designing, Adapting, Strategizing in Online Education

Gunboat and Gun-runner

Meeting Minutes of Naval Lodge No. 4 F.A.A.M ~ 1812 & 1813

Old-World Japan

Legends of the Land of the Gods

by Frank Rinder

WESTPHALIA PRESS
An imprint of Policy Studies Organization

Old-World Japan: Legends of the Land of the Gods
All Rights Reserved © 2014 by Policy Studies Organization

Westphalia Press
An imprint of Policy Studies Organization
1527 New Hampshire Ave., NW
Washington, D.C. 20036
info@ipsonet.org

ISBN-13: 978-1633910508
ISBN-10: 1633910504

Cover design by Taillefer Long at Illuminated Stories:
www.illuminatedstories.com

Daniel Gutierrez-Sandoval, Executive Director
PSO and Westphalia Press

Devin Proctor, Director of Media and Publications
PSO and Westphalia Press

Updated material and comments on this edition
can be found at the Westphalia Press website:
www.westphaliapress.org

OLD-WORLD JAPAN

GEORGE ALLEN

PUBLISHER LONDON

156 CHARING CROSS ROAD

RUSKIN HOUSE

Old-World Japan

Legends of the Land of the
Gods * * Re-told by Frank
Rinder * With Illustrations
by T. H. Robinson

" The spirit of Japan is as the
fragrance of the wild cherry-
blossom in the dawn of the
rising sun "

London: George Allen
156 Charing Cross Road
1895

Preface

HISTORY and mythology, fact and fable, are closely interwoven in the texture of Japanese life and thought; indeed, it is within relatively recent years only that exact comparative criticism has been able, with some degree of accuracy, to divide the one from the other. The accounts of the God-period contained in the Kojiki and the Nihongi—"Records of Ancient Matters" compiled in the eighth century of the Christian era—profess to outline the events of the vast cycles of years from the time of Ame-no-mi-naka-nushi-no-kami's birth in the Plain of High Heaven, "when the earth, young and like unto floating oil, drifted about medusa-like," to the death of the Empress Suiko, A.D. 628.

PREFACE

The first six tales in this little volume are founded on some of the most significant and picturesque incidents of this God-period. The opening legend gives a brief relation of the birth of several of the great Shinto deities, of the creation of Japan and of the world, of the Orpheus-like descent of Izanagi to Hades, and of his subsequent fight with the demons.

That Chinese civilisation has exercised a profound influence on that of Japan, cannot be doubted. A scholar of repute has indicated that evidence of this is to be found even in writings so early as the Kojiki and the Nihongi. To give a single instance only: the curved jewels, of which the remarkable necklace of Ama-terasu was made, have never been found in Japan, whereas the stones are not uncommon in China.

This is not the place critically to consider the wealth of myth, legend, fable, and folk-tale to be found scattered throughout Japanese literature, and represented in Japanese art: suffice it to say, that to the student and the lover of primitive

PREFACE

romance, there are here vast fields practically
unexplored.

The tales contained in this volume have
been selected with a view rather to their
beauty and charm of incident and colour,
than with the aim to represent adequately
the many-sided subject of Japanese lore.
Moreover, those only have been chosen
which are not familiar to the English-read-
ing public. Several of the classic names
of Japan have been interpolated in the text.
It remains to say that, in order not to
weary the reader, it has been found necessary
to abbreviate the many-syllabled Japanese
names.

The sources from which I have drawn
are too numerous to particularise. To Pro-
fessor Basil Hall Chamberlain, whose inti-
mate and scholarly knowledge of all matters
Japanese is well known, my thanks are
especially due, as also the expression of my
indebtedness to other writers in English,
from Mr. A. B. Mitford to Mr. Lafcadio
Hearn, whose volumes on " Unfamiliar Japan "
appeared last year. The careful text of

PREFACE

Dr. David Brauns, and the studies of F. A. Junker von Langegg, have also ,been of great service. The works of numerous French writers on Japanese art have likewise been consulted with advantage.

FRANK RINDER.

Contents

List of Illustrations

LIST OF ILLUSTRATIONS

The Birth-Time

of the Gods

A

The Birth of the Gods

BEFORE time was, and while yet the world was un- created, chaos reigned. The earth and the waters, the light and the darkness, the stars and the firmament, were intermingled in a vapoury liquid. All things were formless and confused. No creature existed; phantom shapes moved as clouds on the ruffled surface of a sea. It was the birth-time of the gods. The first deity sprang from an immense bulrush-bud, which rose, spear-like, in the midst of the boundless disorder. Other gods were born, but three generations passed before the actual separation of the atmosphere from the more solid earth. Finally, where the tip of the bulrush points upward, the Heavenly Spirits appeared.

From this time their kingdom was divided from the lower world where chaos still prevailed. To the fourth pair of gods it was given to create the earth. These two beings were the powerful God of the Air, Izanagi, and the fair Goddess of the Clouds, Izanami. From them sprang all life.

Now Izanagi and Izanami wandered on the Floating Bridge of Heaven. This bridge spanned the gulf between heaven and the unformed world ; it was upheld in the air, and it stood secure. The God of the Air spoke to the Goddess of the Clouds : " There must needs be a kingdom beneath us, let us visit it." When he had so said, he plunged his jewelled spear into the seething mass below. The drops that fell from the point of the spear congealed and became the island of

4

When he had so said, he plunged his jewelled spear into the seething
mass below.

Onogoro. Thereupon the Earth-Makers descended, and called up a high mountain peak, on whose summit could rest one end of the Heavenly Bridge, and around which the whole world should revolve.

The Wisdom of the Heavenly Spirit had decreed that Izanagi should be a man, and Izanami a woman, and these two deities decided to wed and dwell together on the earth. But, as befitted their august birth, the wooing must be solemn. Izanagi skirted the base of the mountain to the right, Izanami turned to the left. When the Goddess of the Clouds saw the God of the Air approaching afar off, she cried, enraptured : "Ah, what a fair and lovely youth!" Then Izanagi exclaimed, "Ah, what a fair and lovely maiden!" As they met, they clasped hands, and the marriage was accomplished. But, for some unknown cause, the union did not prove as happy as the god and goddess had hoped. They continued their work of creation, but Awaji, the island that rose from the deep, was little more than a barren waste, and their first-born son, Hiruko, was a weakling. The Earth-Makers placed him in

7

a little boat woven of reeds, and left him to the mercy of wind and tide.

In deep grief, Izanagi and Izanami recrossed the Floating Bridge, and came to the place where the Heavenly Spirits hold eternal audience. From them they learned that Izanagi should have been the first to speak, when the gods met round the base of the Pillar of Earth. They must woo and wed anew. On their return to earth, Izanagi, as before, went to the right, and Izanami to the left of the mountain, but now, when they met, Izanagi exclaimed : " Ah, what a fair and lovely maiden ! " and Izanami joyfully responded, " Ah, what a fair and lovely youth ! " They clasped hands once more, and their happiness began. They created the eight large islands of the Kingdom of Japan ; first the luxuriant Island of the Dragon-fly, the great Yamato; then Tsukushi, the White-Sun Youth; Iyo, the Lovely Princess, and many more. The rocky islets of the archipelago were formed by the foam of the rolling breakers as they dashed on the coast-lines of the islands already created. Thus China and the remaining lands and continents of the world came into existence.

Now were born to Izanagi and Izanami, the Ruler of the Rivers, the Deity of the Mountains, and, later, the God of the Trees, and a goddess to whom was entrusted the care of tender plants and herbs.

Then Izanagi and Izanami said : "We have created the mighty Kingdom of the Eight Islands, with mountains, rivers, and trees ; yet another divinity there must be, who shall guard and rule this fair world."

As they spoke, a daughter was born to them. Her beauty was dazzling, and her regal bearing betokened that her throne should be set high above the clouds. She was none other than Ama-terasu, The Heaven-Illuminating Spirit. Izanagi and Izanami rejoiced greatly when they beheld her face, and exclaimed, " Our daughter shall dwell in the Blue Plain of High Heaven, and from there she shall direct the universe." So they led her to the summit of the mountain, and over the wondrous bridge. The Heavenly Spirits were joyful when they saw

9

Ama-terasu, and said : "You shall mount into the soft blue of the sky, your brilliancy shall illumine, and your sweet smile shall gladden, the Eternal Land, and all the world. Fleecy clouds shall be your handmaidens, and sparkling dewdrops your messengers of peace."

The next child of Izanagi and Izanami was a son, and as he also was beautiful, with the dream-like beauty of the evening, they placed him in the heavens, as co-ruler with his sister Ama-terasu. His name was Tsuku-yomi, the Moon-God. The god Susa-no-o is another son of the two deities who wooed and wed around the base of the Pillar of Earth. Unlike his brother and his sister, he was fond of the shadow and the gloom. When he wept, the grass on the mountain-side withered, the flowers were blighted, and men died. Izanagi had little joy in this son, nevertheless he made him ruler of the ocean.

Now that the world was created, the happy life of the God of the Air and the Goddess of the Clouds was over. The consumer, the

God of Fire, was born, and Izanami died. She vanished into the deep solitudes of the Kingdom of the Trees, in the country of Kii, and disappeared thence into the lower regions.

Izanagi was sorely troubled because Izanami had been taken from him, and he descended in pursuit of her to the portals of the shadowy kingdom where sunshine is unknown. Izanami would fain have left that place to rejoin Izanagi on the beautiful earth. Her spirit came to meet him, and in urgent and tender words besought him not to seek her in those cavernous regions. But the bold god would not be warned. He pressed forward, and, by the light struck from his comb, he sought for his loved one long and earnestly. Grim forms rose to confront him, but he passed them by with kingly disdain. Sounds as of the wailing of lost souls struck his ear, but still he persisted. After endless search, he found his Izanami lying in an attitude of untold despair, but so changed was she, that he gazed intently into her eyes ere he could recognise her. Izanami was angry that Izanagi had not listened to her commands, for she knew how fruitless would be his efforts. Without the sanction of the ruler of the under-world, she could not return to earth, and this consent she had tried in vain to obtain.

Izanagi, hard pressed by the eight monsters who guard the Land of Gloom, had to flee for his life. He defended himself valiantly with his sword; then he threw down his head-dress, and it was transformed into bunches of purple grapes; he also cast behind him the comb, by means of which he had obtained light, and from it sprang tender shoots of bamboo. While the monsters eagerly devoured the luscious grapes and tender shoots, Izanagi gained the broad flight of steps which led back to earth. At the top he paused and cried to Izanami: "All hope of our reunion is now at an end. Our separation must be eternal."

Stretching far beyond Izanagi lay the ocean, and on its surface was reflected the face of his well-beloved daughter, Ama-terasu. She seemed to speak, and beseech him to purify himself in the great waters of the sea. As he bathed, his wounds were healed, and a sense of infinite peace stole over him.

The life-work of the Earth-Maker was done. He bestowed the world upon his children, and afterwards crossed, for the last time, the many-coloured Bridge of Heaven. The God of the Air now spends his days with the Heaven-Illuminating Spirit in her sun-glorious palace.

The Sun-Goddess

AMA-TERASU, the Sun-Goddess, was
seated in the Blue Plain of Heaven.
Her light came as a message of joy to the
celestial deities. The orchid and the iris, the
cherry and the plum blossom, the rice and
the hemp fields answered to her smile. The
Inland Sea was veiled in soft rich colour.

Susa-no-o, the brother of Ama-terasu, who
had resigned his ocean sceptre and now
reigned as the Moon-God, was jealous of

his sister's glory and world-wide sway. The Heaven-Illuminating Spirit had but to whisper and she was heard throughout her kingdom, even in the depths of the clear pool and in the heart of the crystal. Her rice-fields, whether situated on hill-side, in sheltered valley, or by running stream, yielded abundant harvests, and her groves were laden with fruit. But the voice of Susa-no-o was not so clear, his smile was not so radiant. The undulating fields which lay around his palace were now flooded, now parched, and his rice crops were often destroyed. The wrath and jealousy of the Moon-God knew no bounds, yet Ama-terasu was infinitely patient and forgave him many things.

Once, as was her wont, the Sun-Goddess sat in the central court of her glorious home. She plied her shuttle. Celestial weaving maidens surrounded a fountain whose waters were fragrant with the heavenly lotus-bloom : they sang softly of the clouds and the wind and the lift of the sky. Suddenly, the body of a piebald horse fell through the vast dome at their feet: the " Beloved of the Gods " had been "flayed with a backward flaying" by the envious Susa-no-o. Ama-terasu, trembling at the horrible sight, pricked her finger with the weaving shuttle, and, profoundly indignant at the cruelty of her brother, withdrew into a cave and closed behind her the door of the Heavenly Rock Dwelling.

The universe was plunged in darkness. Joy and goodwill, serenity and peace, hope and love, waned with the waning light. Evil spirits, who heretofore had crouched in dim corners, came forth and roamed abroad. Their grim laughter and discordant tones struck terror into all hearts.

Then it was that the gods, fearful for their safety and for the life of every beautiful thing, assembled in the bed of the tranquil River of Heaven, whose waters had been dried up. One and all knew that Ama-terasu alone could help them. But how allure the Heaven-Illuminating Spirit to set foot in this world of darkness and strife? Each god was eager to aid, and a plan was finally devised to entice her from her hiding-place.

Ame-no-ko uprooted the holy *sakaki* trees

which grow on the Mountain of Heaven,
and planted them around the entrance of the
cave. High on the upper branches were
hung the precious string of curved jewels
which Izanagi had bestowed upon the Sun-
Goddess. From the middle branches drooped
a mirror wrought of the rare metals of the
celestial mine. Its polished surface was as
the dazzling brilliancy of the sun. Other
gods wove, from threads of hemp and paper
mulberry, an imperial robe of white and blue,
which was placed, as an offering for the
goddess, on the lower branches of the *sakaki.*
A palace was also built, surrounded by a
garden in which the Blossom-God called forth
many delicate plants and flowers.

Now all was ready. Ame-no-ko stepped
forward, and, in a loud voice, entreated
Ama - terasu to show herself. His appeal
was in vain. The great festival began.
Uzume, the goddess of mirth, led the dance
and song. Leaves of the spindle tree crowned
her head; club-moss, from the heavenly mount
Kagu, formed her sash; her flowing sleeves
were bound with the creeper-vine; and in her

Ama-terasu gazed into the mirror, and wondered greatly when she
saw therein a goddess of exceeding beauty.

hand she carried leaves of the wild bamboo and waved a wand of sun-grass hung with tiny melodious bells. Uzume blew on a bamboo flute, while the eight hundred myriad deities accompanied her on wooden clappers and instruments formed of bow-strings, across which were rapidly drawn stalks of reed and grass. Great fires were lighted around the cave, and, as these were reflected in the face of the mirror, "the long-singing birds of eternal night" began to crow as if the day dawned. The merriment increased. The dance grew wilder and wilder, and the gods laughed until the heavens shook as if with thunder.

Ama-terasu, in her quiet retreat, heard, unmoved, the crowing of the cocks and the sounds of music and dancing, but when the heavens shook with the laughter of the gods, she peeped from her cave and said : "What means this ? I thought heaven and earth were dark, but now there is light. Uzume dances and all the gods laugh." Uzume answered : " It is true that I dance and that the gods laugh, because in our midst is a

23

goddess whose splendour equals your own. Behold!" Ama-terasu gazed into the mirror, and wondered greatly when she saw therein a goddess of exceeding beauty. She stepped from her cave and forthwith a cord of rice-straw was drawn across the entrance. Darkness fled from the Central Land of Reed-Plains, and there was light. Then the eight hundred myriad deities cried: "O, may the Sun-Goddess never leave us again."

The Heavenly Messengers

The Heavenly Messengers

THE gods looked down from the Plain of
High Heaven and saw that wicked earth-
spirits peopled the lower world. Neither by
day nor by night was there peace. Oshi-homi,
whose name is His Augustness Heavenly-
Great-Great-Ears, was commanded to go
down and govern the earth. As he set foot
on the Floating Bridge, he heard the sounds

of strife and confusion, so he returned, and said, "I would have you choose another deity to do this work." Then the Great Heavenly Spirit and Ama-terasu called together the eight hundred myriad deities in the bed of the Tranquil River of Heaven. The Sun-Goddess spoke: "In the Central Land of Reed-Plains there is trouble and disorder. A deity must descend to prepare the earth for our grandson Prince Ruddy-Plenty, who is to rule over it. Whom shall we send?" The eight hundred myriad deities replied, "Let Ame-no-ho go to the earth."

Now Ame-no-ho descended to the lower world. There he was so happy that the charge of the heavenly deities passed out of his mind. He lived with the earth-spirits, and confusion still reigned.

For three years the Great Heavenly Spirit and Ama-terasu waited for tidings, but none came. Then they said: "We will send Ame-waka, the Heavenly Young Prince. He will surely do our bidding." Into his hands they gave the great heavenly deer-bow and the heavenly feathered arrows which fly straight

28

As the Young Prince alighted on the sea-shore, a beautiful earth-spirit,
Princess Under-Shining, stood before him.

to the mark. "With these you shall war against the wicked earth-spirits, and bring order into the land." But as the Young Prince alighted on the sea-shore, a beautiful earth-spirit, Princess Under-Shining, stood before him. Her loveliness bewitched him. He looked upon her, and could not withdraw his eyes. Soon they were wedded. Eight years passed. The Young Prince spent the time in revelry and feasting. Not once did he attempt to establish peace and order; moreover, he desired to place himself at the head of the earth-spirits, to defy the heavenly deities, and to rule over the Land of Reed-Plains.

Again the eight hundred myriad deities assembled in the bed of the Tranquil River of Heaven. The Sun-Goddess spoke: "Our messenger has tarried in the lower world. Whom shall we send to inquire the cause of this?" Then the gods commanded a faithful pheasant hen: "Go to Ame-waka, and say, 'The Heavenly Deities sent you to the Central Land of Reed-Plains to subdue and pacify the deities of that land. For eight years you have been silent. What is the cause?'" The pheasant flew swiftly to earth, and perched on the branches of a widespreading cassia tree which stood at the gate of the Prince's palace. She spoke every word of her message, but no reply came. Again she repeated the words of the gods, again there was no answer. Now Ama-no-sagu, the Heavenly Spying-Woman, heard the call of the pheasant; she went to the Young Prince, and said, "The cry of this bird bodes ill. Take thy bow and arrows and kill it." Then Ame-waka, in wrath, shot the bird through the heart.

The heavenly arrow fled upward and onward. Swift as the wind it sped through the air, it pierced the clouds and fell at the feet of the Sun-Goddess as she sat on her throne.

Ama-terasu saw that it was one of the arrows that had been entrusted to the Young Prince, and that the feathers were stained with blood. Then she took the arrow in her hands and sent it forth: "If this be an arrow shot by our messenger at the evil spirits, let it not hit the Heavenly Prince. If he has a foul heart, let him perish."

At this moment Ame-waka was resting after the harvest feast. The arrow flew straight to its mark, and pierced him to the heart as he slept. Princess Under-Shining cried aloud when she saw the dead body of the Young Prince. Her cries rose to the heavens. Then the father of Ame-waka raised a mighty storm, and the wind carried the body of the Young Prince to the Blue Plain. A great mourning-house was built, and for eight days and eight nights there was wailing and lamentation. The wild goose of the river, the heron, the kingfisher, the sparrow and the pheasant mourned with a great mourning.

When Aji-shi-ki came to weep for his brother, his face was so like that of the Young Prince that his parents fell upon him, and said : "My child is not dead, no! My lord is not dead, no!" But Aji-shi-ki was wroth because they had taken him for his dead brother. He drew his ten-grasp sabre and cut down the mourning-house, and scattered the fragments to the winds.

Then the heavenly deities said : "Take-Mika shall go down and subdue this unruly land." In company with Tori-bune he set forth and came to the shore of Inasa, in the country of Idzumo. They drew their swords and placed them on a crest of the waves. On the points of the swords Take-Mika and Tori-bune sat, cross-legged : thus they made war against the earth-spirits, and thus subdued them. The land once pacified, their mission was accomplished, and they returned to the Plain of High Heaven.

Prince Ruddy-Plenty

Aᴍᴀ-ᴛᴇʀᴀsᴜ,
    from her sun-glorious
palace, spoke to her grandson,
Ninigi, Prince Rice-Ear-Ruddy-Plenty : " You
must descend from your Heavenly Rock Seat
and go to rule the luxuriant Land-of-Fresh-
Rice-Ears." She gave him many presents ;
precious stones from the mountain steps of
heaven, crystal balls of purest whiteness, and
the cloud-sword which her brother, Susa-no-o,
had drawn from the tail of the terrible dragon.

37

She also entrusted to Ninigi the mirror whose splendour had enticed her from the cave, and said: "Guard this mirror faithfully; when you look into it you shall see my face." A number of deities were commanded to accompany Prince Ruddy-Plenty, among them the beautiful Uzume, who had danced till the heavens shook with the laughter of the gods.

The great company broke through the clouds. Before them, at the eight-forked road of Heaven, stood a deity of gigantic stature, with his large and fiery eyes. The courage of the gods failed at sight of him, and they turned backward. But the fair Uzume went fearlessly up to the giant, and said: "Who is it that thus impedes our descent from heaven?" The deity, well pleased at the gracious mien of the goddess, made answer: "I am a friendly earth-spirit, the Deity of the Field-Paths. I come to meet Ninigi that I may pay homage to him and be his guide. Return and say to the august god that the Prince of Saruta greets him. I am this Prince, O Uzume." The Goddess of Mirth rejoiced greatly when

But the fair Uzume went fearlessly up to the giant, and said : " Who
is it that thus impedes our descent from heaven ? "

she heard these words, and said : " The company of gods shall proceed to earth ; there will Ninigi be made known to you." Then the Deity of the Field-Paths spoke : " Let the army of gods alight on the mountain of Takachihi, in the country of Tsukushi. On its peak I shall await them."

Uzume returned to the gods and delivered the message. When Prince Ruddy-Plenty heard her words he again broke through the eightfold spreading cloud, and floated on the Bridge of Heaven to the summit of Takachihi.

Now Ninigi, with the Prince of Saruta as his guide, travelled throughout the kingdom over which he was to rule. He saw the mountain ranges and the lakes, the great reed plains and the vast pine forests, the rivers and the valleys. Then he said : " It is a land whereon the morning sun shines straight, a land which the evening sun illumines. So this place is an exceeding good place." When he had thus spoken, he built a palace. The pillars rested on the nethermost rock-bottom, and the cross-beams rose to the Plain of High Heaven. In this palace he dwelt.

Again Ninigi spoke: "The God of the Field-Paths shall return to his home. He has been our guide, therefore he shall wed the beautiful goddess, Uzume, and she shall be priestess in his own mountain." Uzume obeyed the commands of Ninigi, and is greatly honoured in Saruta for her courage, her mirth, and her beauty.

It happened that as the Son of the Gods walked along the sea-coast, he saw a maiden of exceeding loveliness. He spoke to her, and said: "By what name are you known?" She replied: "I am the daughter of the Deity Great-Mountain-Possessor, and my name is Ko-no-hane, Princess Tree-Blossom." Ninigi loved the fair Princess. He went to the Spirit of the Mountains, and asked for her hand. But Oho-yama had an elder daughter, Iha-naga, Princess Long-as-the-Rocks, who was less fair than her sister. He desired that the offspring of Prince Ruddy-Plenty should live eternally like unto the rocks, and flourish as the blossom of the trees. Therefore

Oho-yama sent both his daughters to Ninigi in rich attire and with many rare presents. Ninigi loved the beautiful Princess Ko-no-hane. He would not look upon Iha-naga. She cried out in wrath: "Had you chosen me, you and your children would have lived long on earth ; but as you love my sister all your descendants will perish rapidly as the blossom of the trees." Thus it is that human life is so short compared with that of the earlier peoples that were gods.

For some time, Ninigi dwelt happily with Princess Tree-Blossom : then a cloud came over their lives. Ko-no-hane had the delicate grace, the morning freshness, the subtle charm of the cherry blossom. She loved the sun-shine and the soft west wind. She loved the cool rain, and the quiet summer night. But Ninigi grew jealous. In anger Princess Tree-Blossom retired to her palace, closed up the entrance, and set it on fire. The flames rose higher and higher. Ninigi watched anxiously. As he looked, three little boys sprang merrily out of the flames and called for their father. Prince Ruddy-Plenty was

43

glad once more, and when he saw Ko-no-hane, unharmed, move towards him, he asked her forgiveness. They named their sons Ho-deri, Fire-Flash; Ho-suseri, Fire-Climax; and Ho-wori, Fire-Fade.

After many years, Ninigi divided his kingdom between two of his sons. Then Prince Ruddy-Plenty returned to the Plain of High Heaven.

The Palace of

the Ocean-Bed

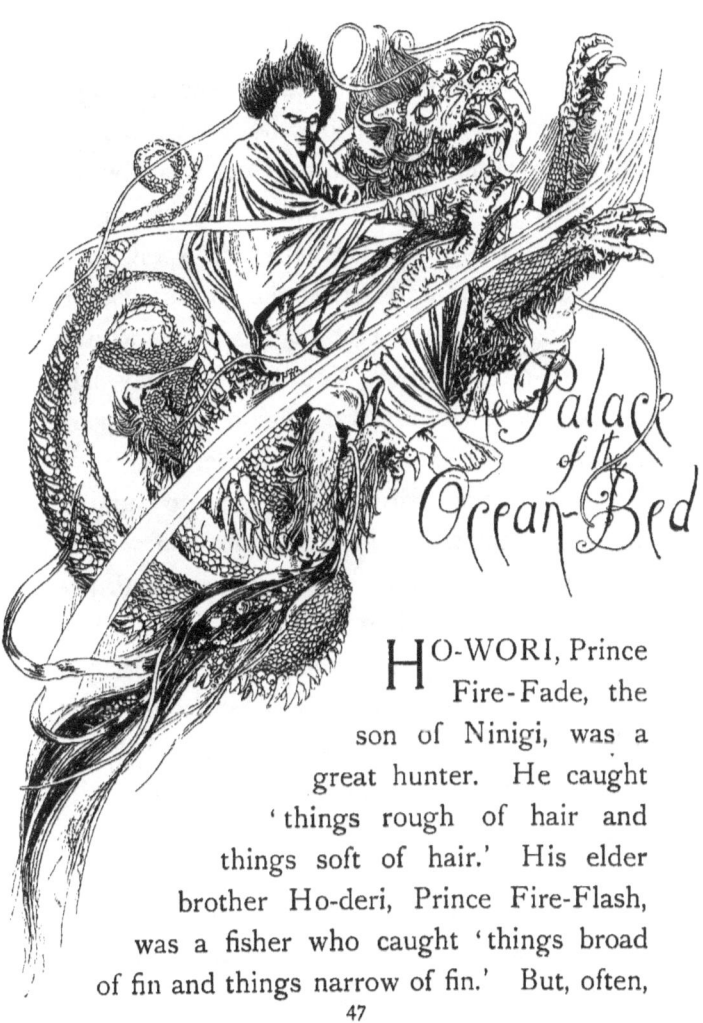

The Palace of the Ocean-Bed

HO-WORI, Prince Fire-Fade, the son of Ninigi, was a great hunter. He caught 'things rough of hair and things soft of hair.' His elder brother Ho-deri, Prince Fire-Flash, was a fisher who caught 'things broad of fin and things narrow of fin.' But, often,

47

when the wind blew and the waves ran high, he would spend hours on the sea and catch no fish. When the Storm God was abroad, Ho-deri had to stay at home, while at nightfall Ho-wori returned laden with spoil from the mountains. Ho-deri spoke to his brother, and said : " I would have your bow and arrows and become a hunter. You shall have my fish-hook." At first Ho-wori would not consent, but finally the exchange was made.

Now Prince Fire - Flash was no hunter. He could not track the game, nor run swiftly, nor take good aim. Day after day Prince Fire-Fade went out to sea. In vain he threw his line ; he caught no fish. Moreover, one day, he lost his brother's fish-hook. Then Ho-deri came to Ho-wori, and said : " There is the luck of the mountain and there is the luck of the sea. Let each restore to the other his luck." Ho-wori replied : " I did not catch a single fish with your hook, and now it is lost in the sea." The elder brother was very angry, and, with many hard words, demanded the return of his treasure. Prince Fire-Fade was unhappy. He broke in pieces his good sword and made five hundred fish-hooks which he offered to his brother. But this did not appease the wrath of Prince Fire-Flash, who still raged and asked for his own hook.

Ho-wori could find neither comfort nor help. He sat one day by the shore and heaved a deep sigh. The old Man of the Sea heard the sigh, and asked the cause of his sorrow. Ho-wori told him of the loss of the fish-hook, and of his brother's displeasure. Thereupon the wise man promised to give his help. He plaited strips of bamboo so tightly together that the water could not pass through, and fashioned therewith a stout little boat. Into this boat Ho-wori jumped, and was carried far out to sea.

After a time, as the old man had foretold, his boat began to sink. Deeper and deeper it sank, until at last he came to a glittering palace of fishes' scales. In front of it was a well, shaded by a great cassia tree. Prince Fire - Fade sat among the wide - spreading branches. He looked down, and saw a maiden approach the well; in her hand she car- ried a jewelled bowl. She was the lovely

Toyo-tama, Peerless Jewel, the daughter of Wata-tsu-mi, the Sea-King. Ho-wori was spell-bound by her strange wave-like beauty, her long flowing hair, her soft deep blue eyes. The maiden stooped to fill her bowl. Suddenly, she saw the reflection of Prince Fire-Fade in the water; she dropped the precious bowl, and it fell in a thousand pieces. Toyo-tama hastened to her father, and exclaimed, "A man, with the grace and beauty of a god, sits in the branches of the cassia tree. I have seen his picture in the waters of the well." The Sea-King knew that it must be the great hunter, Prince Fire-Fade.

Then Wata-tsu-mi went forth and stood under the cassia tree. He looked up to Ho-wori, and said: "Come down, O Son of the Gods, and enter my Palace of the Ocean-Bed." Ho-wori obeyed, and was led into the palace and seated on a throne of sea-asses' skins. A banquet was prepared in his honour. The *hashi* were delicate branches of coral, and the plates were of silvery mother-of-pearl. The clear-rock wine was sipped from cup-shaped ocean blooms with long

Suddenly, she saw the reflection of Prince Fire-Fade in the water.

slender stalks. Ho-wori thought that never before had there been such a banquet. When it was ended he went with Toyo-tama to the roof of the palace. Dimly, through the blue waters that moved above, he could discern the Sun-Goddess. He saw the mountains and valleys of ocean, the waving forests of tall sea-plants, the homes of the *shaké* and the *kani*.

Ho-wori told Wata-tsu-mi of the loss of the fish-hook. Then the Sea-King called all his subjects together and questioned them. No fish knew aught of the hook, but, said the lobster: "As I sat one day in my crevice among the rocks, the *tai* passed near me. His mouth was swollen, and he went by without giving me greeting." Wata-tsu-mi then noticed that the *tai* had not answered his summons. A messenger, fleet of fin, was sent to fetch him. When the *tai* appeared, the lost fish-hook was found in his poor wounded mouth. It was restored to Ho-wori, and he was happy. Toyo-tama became his bride, and they lived together in the cool fish-scale palace.

Prince Fire-Fade came to understand the secrets of the ocean, the cause of its anger, the cause of its joy. The Storm-Spirit of the upper sea did not rule in the ocean-bed, and night after night Ho-wori was rocked to sleep by the gentle motion of the waters.

Many tides had ebbed and flowed, when, in the quiet of the night, Ho-wori heaved a deep sigh. Toyo-tama was troubled, and told her father that, as Ho-wori dreamt of his home on the earth, a great longing had come over him to visit it once more. Then Wata-tsu-mi gave into Ho-wori's hands two great jewels, the one to rule the flow, the other to rule the ebb of the tide. He spoke thus: "Return to earth on the head of my trusted sea-dragon. Restore the lost fish-hook to Ho-deri. If he is still wroth with you, bring forth the tide-flowing jewel, and the waters shall cover him. If he asks your forgiveness, bring forth the tide-ebbing jewel, and it shall be well with him."

Ho-wori left the Palace of the Ocean-Bed, and was carried swiftly to his own land.

As he set foot on the shore, he ungirded his sword, and tied it round the neck of the sea-dragon. Then he said: "Take this to the Sea-King as a token of my love and gratitude."

Autumn and Spring

A FAIR maiden lay asleep in a rice-field. The sun was at its height, and she was weary. Now a god looked down upon the rice-field. He knew that the beauty of the maiden came from within, that it mirrored the beauty of heavenly dreams. He knew that even now, as she smiled, she held converse with the spirit of the wind or the flowers.

The god descended and asked the dream-maiden to be his bride. She rejoiced, and they were wed. A wonderful red jewel came of their happiness.

Long, long afterwards, the stone was found by a farmer, who saw that it was a very rare jewel. He prized it highly, and always carried it about with him. Sometimes, as he looked at it in the pale light of the moon, it seemed to him that he could discern two sparkling eyes in its depths. Again, in the stillness of the night, he would awaken and think that a clear soft voice called him by name.

One day, the farmer had to carry the mid-day meal to his workers in the field. The sun was very hot, so he loaded a cow with the bowls of rice, the millet dumplings, and the beans. Suddenly, Prince Ama-boko stood in the path. He was angry, for he thought that the farmer was about to kill the cow. The Prince would hear no word of denial; his wrath increased. The farmer became more and more terrified, and, finally, took the precious stone from his pocket and presented it as a peace-offering to the powerful Prince. Ama-boko marvelled at the brilliancy of the jewel, and allowed the man to continue his journey.

The Prince returned to his home. He drew forth the treasure, and it was immediately transformed into a goddess of surpassing beauty. Even as she rose before him, he loved her, and ere the moon waned they were wed. The goddess ministered to his every want. She prepared delicate dishes, the secret of which is known only to the gods. She made wine from the juice of a myriad herbs, wine such as mortals never taste.

But, after a time, the Prince became proud and overbearing. He began to treat his faithful wife with cruel contempt. The goddess was sad, and said: "You are not worthy of my love. I will leave you and go to my father." Ama-boko paid no heed to these words, for he did not believe that the threat would be fulfilled. But the beautiful goddess was in earnest. She escaped from the palace and fled to Naniwa, where she is still honoured as Akaru-hime, the Goddess of Light.

Now the Prince was wroth when he heard that the goddess had left him, and set out in pursuit of her. But when he neared Naniwa, the gods would not allow his vessel to enter the haven. Then he knew that his priceless red jewel was lost to him for ever. He steered his ship towards the north coast of Japan, and landed at Tajima. Here he was well received, and highly esteemed on account of the treasures which he brought with him. He had costly strings of pearls, girdles of precious stones, and a mirror which the wind and the waves obeyed. Prince Ama-boko remained at Tajima, and was the father of a mighty race.

Among his children's children was a princess so renowned for her beauty that eighty suitors sought her hand. One after the other returned sorrowfully home, for none found favour in her eyes. At last, two brothers came before her, the young God of the Autumn, and the young God of the Spring. The elder of the two, the God of Autumn, first urged his suit. But the princess refused him. He went to his younger brother, and said : " The princess does not

One after the other returned sorrowfully home, for none found favour
in her eyes.

love me, neither will you be able to win her
heart." But the Spring God was full of hope,
and replied: "I will give you a cask of rice
wine if I do not win her, but if she consents
to be my bride, you shall give a cask of *saké*
to me."

Now the God of Spring went to his mother,
and told her all. She promised to aid him.
Thereupon she wove, in a single night, a robe
and sandals from the unopened buds of the
lilac and white wisteria. Out of the same
delicate flowers she fashioned a bow and
arrows. Thus clad, the God of Spring made
his way to the beautiful princess.

As he stepped before the maiden, every bud
unfolded, and from the heart of each blossom
came a fragrance that filled the air. The
princess was overjoyed, and gave her hand to
the God of the Spring.

The elder brother, the God of Autumn, was
filled with rage when he heard how his brother
had obtained the wondrous robe. He refused
to give the promised cask of *saké*. When the
mother learned that the god had broken his
word, she placed stones and salt in the hollow

of a bamboo cane, wrapped it round with bamboo leaves, and hung it in the smoke. Then she uttered a curse upon her first-born son : " As the leaves wither and fade, so must you. As the salt sea ebbs, so must you. As the stone sinks, so must you."

The terrible curse fell upon her son. While the God of Spring remains ever young, ever fragrant, ever full of mirth, the God of Autumn is old, and withered, and sad.

The Star-Lovers

The Star Lovers

HOKUJO, daughter of the Sun, dwelt with her father on the banks of the Silver River of Heaven, which we call the Milky Way. She was a lovely maiden, graceful and winsome, and her eyes were tender as the eyes of a dove. Her loving father, the Sun, was much troubled because Shokujo did not share in the youthful pleasures of the daughters of the air. A soft melancholy seemed to brood over her, but she never wearied of working

69

for the good of others, and especially did she busy herself at her loom; indeed she came to be called the Weaving Princess.

The Sun bethought him, that if he could give his daughter in marriage, all would be well; her dormant love would be kindled into a flame that would illumine her whole being and drive out the pensive spirit which oppressed her. Now there lived, hard by, one Kingen, a right honest herdsman, who tended his cows on the borders of the Heavenly Stream. The Sun-King proposed to bestow his daughter on Kingen, thinking in this way to provide for her happiness and at the same time to keep her near him. Every star beamed approval, and there was joy in the heavens.

The love that bound Shokujo and Kingen to one another was a great love. With its awakening, Shokujo forsook her former occupations, nor did she any longer labour industriously at the loom, but laughed, and danced, and sang, and made merry from morn till night. The Sun-King was sorely grieved, for he had not foreseen so great a change. Anger

The lovers were wont, standing on the banks of the celestial stream, to waft across it sweet and tender messages.

was in his eyes, and he said, "Kingen is surely the cause of this, therefore I will banish him to the other side of the River of Stars."

When Shokujo and Kingen heard that they were to be parted, and could thenceforth, in accordance with the King's decree, meet but once a year, and that upon the seventh night of the seventh month, their hearts were heavy. The leave-taking between them was a sad one, and great tears stood in Shokujo's eyes as she bade farewell to her lover-husband. In answer to the behest of the Sun-King, myriads of magpies flocked together, and, outspreading their wings, formed a bridge, on which Kingen crossed the River of Heaven. The moment that his foot touched the opposite bank, the birds dispersed with noisy chatter, leaving poor Kingen a solitary exile. He looked wistfully towards the weeping figure of Shokujo, who stood on the threshold of her now desolate home.

Long and weary were the succeeding days, spent as they were by Kingen in guiding his oxen and by Shokujo in plying her shuttle.

The Sun-King was gladdened by his daughter's industry. When night fell and the heavens were bright with countless lights, the lovers were wont, standing on the banks of the celestial stream, to waft across it sweet and tender messages, while each uttered a prayer for the speedy coming of the wondrous night.

The long-hoped-for month and day drew nigh, and the hearts of the lovers were troubled lest rain should fall : for the Silver River, full at all times, is at that season often in flood, and the bird-bridge might be swept away.

The day broke cloudlessly bright. It waxed and waned, and one by one the lamps of heaven were lighted. At nightfall the magpies assembled, and Shokujo, quivering with delight, crossed the slender bridge and fell into the arms of her lover. Their transport of joy was as the joy of the parched flower, when the raindrop falls upon it ; but the moment of parting soon came, and Shokujo sorrowfully retraced her steps.

Year follows year, and the lovers still meet in that far-off starry land on the seventh night of the seventh month, save when rain has swelled the Silver River and rendered the crossing impossible. The hope of a permanent reunion still fills the hearts of the Star-Lovers, and is to them as a sweet fragrance and a beautiful vision.

The Island of

Eternal Youth

The Island of Eternal Youth

F AR beyond the faint grey of the horizon, somewhere in the shadowy Unknown, lies the Island of Eternal Youth. The dwellers on the rocky coast of the East Sea of Japan relate that, at times, a wondrous tree can be discerned rising high above the waves. It is the tree which has stood for all ages on the loftiest peak of Fusan, the Mountain of Immortality. Men rejoice when they catch a glimpse of its branches, though the glimpse be fleeting as a vision at dawn. On the island is endless spring : the air is ever sweet and the sky blue. Celestial dews fall softly upon every tree and flower, and carry with them the secret of eternity. The delicate white bryony never loses its first-day freshness, the scarlet lily cannot fade. Ethereal pink blossoms enfold the branches of the *sakuranoki*; the pendulous fruit of the orange bears no trace of age. Irises, violet and yellow and blue, fringe the pool on whose surface float the heavenly-coloured lotus blooms. From day to day the birds sing of love and joy. Sorrow and pain are unknown, death comes not hither. The Spirit of this island it is who whispers to the sleeping Spring in every land, and bids her arise.

Many brave seafarers have sought Horaizan but have not reached its shores. Some have suffered shipwreck in the attempt, others have mistaken the heights of Fuji-yama for the blessed Fusan.

Now there once lived a cruel Emperor of China. So tyrannical was he that the life of his physician, Jofuku, was in constant danger. One day, Jofuku spoke to the Emperor, and said : "Give me a ship, and I will sail to the

Island of Eternal Youth. There I will pluck the herb of immortality and bring it back to you, that you may rule over your kingdom for ever." The despot heard the words with pleasure. Jofuku, fully equipped, set sail and came to Japan; thence he steered his course towards the magic tree. Days, months, and years passed. Jofuku seemed to be drifting on the ocean of heaven, for no land was visible. At last, far in the distance, rose the dim outline of a hill such as he had never seen before; and when he perceived a tree on its summit, Jofuku knew that he neared Horai-zan. Soon he came to its shores, and landed as one in a dream. Every thought of the Emperor, whose days were to be prolonged by eating of the sacred herb, passed from his mind. Life upon the beautiful island was so glorious that he had no wish to return. His story is told by Wasobiowe, a wise man of Japan, who, alone among mortals, can relate the wonders of that strange land.

Wasobiowe dwelt in the neighbourhood of Nagasaki. He loved nothing better than to spend his days far out at sea, fishing from a

little boat. Once, when the eighth full moon
rose—which in Japan is called the "bean
moon" and is the most beautiful of all—
Wasobiowe started on a long voyage in
order to be absent from Nagasaki during the
festivals of the season. Leisurely he skirted
the coast, and rejoiced in the bold outlines
of the rocks seen by the light of the moon.
But, without warning, black clouds gathered
overhead. The storm burst, the rain poured
down, and darkness fell. The waves were
lashed into fury, and the little boat was
driven swift as an arrow before the wind.
For three days and nights the hurricane
raged. As dawn broke on the fourth morning, the wind was stilled, the sea grew calm.
Wasobiowe, who knew the course of the stars,
saw that he was far from his home in Japan.
He was at the mercy of the god of the tides.
For months Wasobiowe ate the fish which he
caught in his net, until his boat drifted into
those black waters where no fish can live.
He rowed and rowed ; his strength was
almost spent. Hope had left him, when, suddenly, a fragrant wind from the land played

Soon he came to its shores, and landed as one in a dream.

about his temples. He seized the oars, and soon his boat reached the coast of Horaizan. Even as he landed, all remembrance of the dangers and privations of the voyage vanished.

Everything spoke of joy and sunlight. The hum of the cicala, the whirr of the darting dragon-fly, the call of the bright-green tree-frog sounded in his ear. Sweet scents came from the pine-covered hills ; everywhere was a flood of glowing colour.

Presently a man approached him. It was none other than Jofuku. He spoke to Wasobiowe, and told how the elect of the gods, who peopled those remote shores, filled their days with music and laughter and song.

Wasobiowe lived contentedly on the Island of Eternal Youth. He knew nothing of the flight of years, for where there is no birth, no death, time passes unheeded.

But, after many hundred years, the wise man of Nagasaki wearied of this blissful existence. He longed for death, but the dark river does not flow through Horaizan. He would wistfully follow the outward flight of the birds, till they became mere specks in the sky. One day he spoke to a pure white stork : " I know that the birds alone can leave this island. Carry me, I pray you, to my home in Japan. I would see it once more and die." Then he mounted upon the outstretched wings of the stork, and was carried across the sea and through many strange lands, peopled by giants and dwarfs and men with white faces. When he had visited all the countries of the earth, he came to his beloved Japan. In his hand he bore a branch of the orange which he planted. The tree still flourishes in the Mikado's Empire.

Rai-Taro, the Son

of the Thunder-God

Rai-Taro, the Son of the Thunder God

A T the
foot of the
snowy mountain of
Haku-san, in the pro-
vince of Echizen, lived a peasant and his
wife. They were very poor, for their little
strip of barren mountain-land yielded but

89

one scanty crop a year, while their neighbours in the valley gathered two rich harvests.
With unceasing patience, Bimbo worked from
cock - crow until the barking of the foxes
warned him that night had fallen. He laid
out his plot of ground in terraces, surrounded
them with dams, and diverted the course of
the mountain stream that it might flood his
fields. But when no rain came to swell
the brook, Bimbo's harvest failed. Often as
he sat in his hut with his wife, after a long
day of hard work, he would speak of their
troubles. The peasants were filled with grief
that a child had not been given to them.
They longed to adopt a son, but, as they had
barely enough for their own simple wants, the
dream could not be realised.

An evil day came when the land of Echizen
was parched. No rain fell. The brook was
dried up. The young rice-sprouts withered.
Bimbo sighed heavily over his work. He
looked up to the sky and entreated the gods
to take pity on him.

After many weeks of sunshine, the sky was
overcast. Single clouds came up rapidly

from the west, and gathered in angry masses.
A strange silence filled the air. Even the
voice of the cicalas, who had chirped in the
trees during the heat of the day, was stilled.
Only the cry of the mountain hawk was
audible. A murmur passed over valley and
hill, a faint rustling of leaves, a whispering
sigh in the needles of the fir. Fu-ten, the
Storm-Spirit, and Rai-den, the Thunder-God,
were abroad. Deeper and deeper sank the
clouds under the weight of the thunder dragon.
The rain came at first in large cool drops,
then in torrents.

Bimbo rejoiced, and worked steadily to
strengthen the dams and open the conduits
of his farm.

A vivid flash of lightning, a mighty roar of
thunder! Terrified, almost blinded, Bimbo fell
on his knees. He thought that the claws of
the thunder dragon were about him. But he
was unharmed, and he offered thanks to
Kwan-non, the Goddess of Pity, who pro-
tects mortals from the wrath of the Thunder-
God. On the spot where the lightning struck
the ground, lay a little rosy boy full of life,

who held out his arms and lisped. Bimbo was greatly amazed, and his heart was glad, for he knew that the gods had heard and answered his never-uttered prayer. The happy peasant took the child up, and carried him under his rice-straw coat to the hut. He called to his wife, " Rejoice, our wish is fulfilled. The gods have sent us a child. We will call him Rai-taro, the Son of the Thunder-God, and bring him up as our own."

The good woman fondly tended the boy. Rai-taro loved his foster-parents, and grew up dutiful and obedient. He did not care to play with other children, but was always happy to work in the fields with Bimbo, where he would watch the flight of the birds, and listen to the sound of the wind. Long before Bimbo could discern any sign of an approaching storm, Rai-taro knew that it was at hand. When it drew near, he fixed his eyes intently on the gathering clouds, he listened eagerly to the roll of the thunder, the rush of the rain, and he greeted each flash of lightning with a shout of joy.

Rai-taro had come as a ray of sunshine

The birth of Rai-taro.

into the lives of the poor peasants. Good fortune followed the farmer from the day that he carried the little boy home in his rain-coat. The mountain stream was never dry. The land was fertile, and he gathered rich harvests of rice and abundant crops of millet. Year by year, his prosperity increased, until from Bimbo, 'the poor,' he became Kane-mochi, 'the prosperous.'

About eighteen summers passed, and Rai-taro still lived with his foster-parents. Sud-denly, they knew not why, he became thought-ful and sad. Nothing would rouse him. The peasants determined to hold a feast in honour of his birthday. They called together the neighbours, and there was much rejoicing. Bimbo told many tales of other days, and, finally, of how Rai-taro came to him out of the storm. As he ceased, a strange far-off look was in the eyes of the Son of the Thunder-God. He stood before his foster-parents, and said: "You have loved me well. You have been faithful and kind. But the time has come for me to leave you. Farewell."

In a moment Rai-taro was gone. A white cloud floated upward towards the heights of Haku-san. As it neared the summit of the mountain, it took the form of a white dragon. Higher still the dragon soared, until, at last, it vanished into a castle of clouds.

The peasants looked wistfully up to the sky. They hoped that Rai-taro might return, but he had joined his father, Rai-den, the Thunder-God, and was seen no more.

The Souls of

the Children

The Souls of the Children

SAI-NO-KAWARA, the Dry Bed of the River of Souls. Far below the roots of the mountains, far below the bottom of the sea is the course of this river. Ages ago its current bore the souls of the blessed dead to the Land of Eternal Peace. The wicked *oni* were angry when they saw the good spirits pass out of their reach on the breast of the river. They muttered curses in their throats as the stream flowed on day by day, year by year. The snow-white soul of a

99

tender child came to the bank. A cup-shaped lotus bloom waited to carry the little one swiftly, through the dark cavernous region, to the kingdom of joy. The *oni* gnashed their teeth. The spirit of a kindly old man, whose heart was young, would thread his way unharmed, through the horde of demons, and float on the Heavenly-Bird-Boat to the unknown world. The *oni* looked on in wrath.

But the *oni* stemmed the River of Souls at its source, and now the spirits of the dead must wend their way, unaided, to the country that lies far beyond.

Jizo, The Never-Slumbering, is the god who guards the souls of little children. He is full of pity, his voice is gentle as the voice of the doves on Mount Hasa, his love is infinite as the waters of the sea. To him every child in the Land of the Gods calls for succour and protection.

In Sai-no-Kawara, The Dry Bed of the River of Souls, are the spirits of countless children. Babes of two and three years old, babes of four and five, children of eight and ten. Their wailing is pitiful to hear. They

cry for the mother who bore them. They cry
for the father who cherished them. They
cry for the brother and sister whom they
love. Their cry is heard throughout Sai-no-
Kawara, a cry that rises and falls, and falls
and rises, rhythmic, unceasing. These are
the words that they cry—

"Chichi koishi! haha koishi!——"

Their voices grow hoarse as they cry, and
still they cry on—

"Chichi koishi! haha koishi!——"

While day lasts, they cry and they gather
stones from the bed of the river, and heap
them together as prayers.

A Tower of Prayer for the sweet mother,
as they cry:

A Tower of Prayer for the father, as they cry:

A Tower of Prayer for brother and sister,
as they cry:

From morning till evening they cry—

"Chichi koishi! haha koishi!——"
and heap up the stones of prayer.

At nightfall come the *oni*, the demons, and
say: "Why do you cry, why do you pray?
Your parents in the Shaba-World cannot hear

you. Your prayers are lost in the strife of tongues. The lamentation of your parents on earth is the cause of all your sorrow." So saying, the wicked *oni* cast down the Towers of Prayer, every one, and dash the stones into great caverns of the rocks.

But Jizo, with a great love in his eyes, comes and enfolds the little ones in his robe. To the babes who cannot walk, he stretches forth his *shakujo*. The children in Sai-no-Kawara gather round him, and he speaks sweet words of comfort. He lifts them in his arms and caresses them, for Jizo is father and mother to the little ones who dwell in the Dry Bed of the River of Souls.

Then they cease from their crying: they cease to build the Towers of Prayer. Night has come, and the souls of the children sleep peacefully, while The Never-Slumbering Jizo watches over them.

The Moon-Maiden

The Moon Maiden

IT was early spring on the coast of Suruga. Tender green flushed the bamboo thickets. A rose-tinged cloud from heaven had fallen softly on the branches of the cherry tree. The pine forests were fragrant of the spring. Save for the lap of the sea, there was silence on that remote shore.

A far-off sound became audible : it might be

the song of falling waters, it might be the
voice of the awakening wind, it might be the
melody of the clouds. The strange sweet
music rose and fell : the cadence was as the
cadence of the sea. Slowly, imperceptibly,
the music came nearer.

Above the lofty heights of Fuji-yama a
snow-white cloud floated earthwards. Nearer
and nearer came the music. A low clear
voice could be heard chanting a lay that
breathed of the peace and tranquillity of the
moonlight. The fleecy cloud was borne towards the shore. For one moment it seemed
to rest upon the sand, and then it melted
away.

By the sea stood a glistening maiden. In
her hand she carried a heart-shaped instrument, and, as her fingers touched the strings,
she sang a heavenly song. She wore a robe
of feathers, white and spotless as the breast of
the wild swan. The maiden looked at the sea.
Then she moved towards the belt of pine trees
that fringed the shore. Birds flocked around
her ; they perched on her shoulder, and
rubbed their soft heads against her cheek.

She stroked them gently and they flew away full of joy. The maiden hung her robe of feathers on a pine branch, and went to bathe in the sea.

It was mid-day. A fisher sat down among the pines to eat his dumpling. Suddenly, his eye fell on the dazzling white robe. " Perhaps it is a gift from the gods," said Hairukoo as he went up to it. The robe was so fragile that he almost feared to touch it, but at last he took it down. The feathers were wondrously woven together, and slender curved wings sprang from above the shoulder. " I will take it home, and we shall be happy," he thought.

Now the maiden came from the sea. Hairukoo heard no sound until she stood before him. Then a soft voice spoke : " The robe is mine, good fisher, pray give it to me." The man stood awestruck, for never had he seen so lovely a being. She seemed to come from another world. He said, " What is your name, beautiful maiden, and whence do you come? " She answered, " I am one of the virgins who attend the moon. I come with a message of peace to the ocean. I have whispered it into his ear, and now I must fly heavenward." But Hairukoo replied, "I would see you dance before you leave me." The moon-maiden answered: "Give me my feather robe, and I will dance a celestial dance." The peasant refused. "Dance and I will give you your robe." Then the glittering virgin was angry: "The wicked *oni* will take you for their own, if you doubt the word of a goddess. I cannot dance without my robe. Each feather has been given to me by the Heavenly Birds. Their love and trust support me." As she thus spoke the fisher was ashamed, and said, "I have done wrong, and I ask your forgiveness." Then he gave the robe into her hands. The moon-maiden put it around her.

And now she rose from the ground. She touched the stringed instrument and sang. Clear and infinitely sweet came the notes. It was her farewell to the earth and the sea. It ceased. She broke into a merry trilling song, and began to dance. At one moment she skimmed the surface of the sea, the next her tiny feet touched the topmost branches of

At one moment she skimmed the surface of the sea, the next her tiny feet
touched the topmost branches of the tall pine trees.

the tall pine trees. Then she sped past the
fisher and smiled as the long grass rustled
beneath her. She swept through the air, in
and out among the trees, over the bamboo
thicket, and under the branches of the blossom-
ing cherry. Still the music went on. Still
the maiden danced. Hairukoo looked on in
wonder : he thought it must all be a beautiful
dream.

But now the music changed. It was no
longer merry. The dance ended. The maiden
sang of the moonlight, and of the quiet of
evening.

She began to circle in the air. Slowly at
first, then more swiftly, she floated over the
woods towards the distant mountain. The
music and the song rang in the ears of the
fisher. The maiden was wafted farther and
farther away. Hairukoo watched until he
could no longer discern her snow-white form
in the sky. But still the music reached him on
the breeze. At last it too died away. The
fisher was left alone : alone with the sound
of the sea, and the fragrance of the pines.

The Great Fir Tree
of Takasago

The Great Fir Tree of Takasago

THE cherry tree has blossomed many times since O-Matsue lived with her father and mother on the sandy coast of the Inland Sea. The home at Takasago was sheltered by a tall fir tree of great age; a god had planted it as he passed that way. O-Matsue was beautiful, for her mother had taught her to love the sea, and the birds, the trees, and every living thing.

115

Her eyes were like a clear deep ocean-pool on a summer day. Her smile was as the sunshine on the surface of Lake Biwa.

The fallen needles of the fir made a soft couch on which O-Matsue sat for hours at a time, plying her shuttle, weaving robes for the peasants around. Sometimes, she would go to sea with the fishers, and peer into the depths to try and catch a glimpse of the Palace of the Ocean Bed ; the fishers would tell her the story of the poor jelly-fish who lost his shell, or of the Blessed Island of Eternal Youth, whose tree could at times be discerned from the coast.

The steep shore of Sumi-no-ye is many leagues distant from Takasago, but a youth who dwelt there took a long journey. Teoyo said, " I will see what lies beyond the mountains. I will see the country to which the heron wings his way across the plain." He travelled through many provinces, and at last came to the land of Harima. One day he passed by Takasago. O-Matsue sat in the shade of the fir tree. She was weaving, and sang as she worked. These are the words of her song :—

> " No man so callous but he heaves a sigh
>   When o'er his head the withered Cherry flowers
>   Come fluttering down. Who knows? the Spring's
>   soft showers
>   May be but tears shed by the sorrowing sky."

Teoyo heard the sweet song, and said. "It is like the song of a spirit,—and how beautiful the maiden is!" For some time he watched her as she wove. Then her song ceased, he moved towards her, and spoke: "I have travelled far. I have seen many fair maidens, but not one so fair as you. Take me to your father and mother that I may speak with them." Teoyo asked the peasants for the hand of their daughter, and they gave their consent.

There was great rejoicing. O-Matsue received many presents, and, as the wedding-day approached, a great feast was prepared. Bride and bridegroom drank thrice of three cups of *saké* which made them man and wife, and the feast went on.

Now Teoyo said, "This country of Harima

117

is a good land. Let us stay here with your father and mother." O-Matsue was glad. So they dwelt with the old people under the great fir tree. At last, the father and mother died. O-Matsue and Teoyo still lived beneath the shelter of the tree. They were very happy. Summer, autumn and winter passed over the land of Harima many times. Their love was always in its spring. The "waves of age" furrowed their brows, but their hearts remained young and tender, green as the needles of the pine. Even when their eyes had grown dim, they went to the shore to listen to the waters of the Inland Sea, or together they gathered, with rakes of bamboo, the fallen needles of the fir.

A crane came and built in the topmost branches of the tree, and for many years they watched the birds rear their young. A tortoise also dwelt beside them. O-Matsue said, "We are blessed with a fir tree, a crane, and a tortoise. The God of Long Life has taken us under his care."

When, at last, at the same moment, Teoyo and O-Matsue died, their spirits withdrew into the tree which had for so long been the witness of their happiness. To this day the pine tree is called " The Pine of the Lovers."

On moonbright nights, when the coast wind whispers in the branches of the tree, O-Matsue and Teoyo may sometimes be seen, with bamboo rakes in their hands, gathering together the needles of the fir.

Despite the storms of time, the old tree stands to this hour eternally green on the high shore of Takasago.

The Willow of
Mukochima

The Willow of Mukochima

NOT far from Matsue, the great city of the Province of the Gods, there once dwelt a widow and her son. Their wooden hut looked upon the Shinji Lake set in a framework of mountain peaks. Ayame was true to the old religion, the worship of the descendants of Izanagi and Izanami. Long ere the sun rose above the chain of hills, she was up, and, with Umewaki's hand clasped closely in her own, went down to the verge of the lake. First they laved their faces in the cool water, then, turning towards the east, they clapped their hands four times and saluted the sun. "Konnichi Sama! All hail to thee, Day-Maker. Shine and bring joy to the Place of the Issuing of Clouds." Then, having turned towards the west, mother and son blessed the holy, immemorial shrine of Kitzuki; towards the north and the south they turned and prayed to the gods, unto each one, who dwell in the blue Plain of High Heaven.

Umewaki's father had been dead many years, and the love of the mother was centred upon her son. He was in the open air from sunrise to nightfall; sometimes by Ayame's side, sometimes alone, watching the heron or the crane, or listening to the sweet call of the *yamabato*. The hut was in a remote spot, but Ayame felt that her son was safe in the keeping of the good gods.

It was a beautiful summer morning. Ayame and Umewaki awakened soon after dawn. Hand in hand they went to the shore of Lake Shinji. It still slept beneath the faintly-tinged haze. The Lady of Fire had not whispered of her approach to the soft mists that veiled the hills. Mother and son waited patiently. As the Day-Maker appeared, they cried, " Konnichi Sama! Great Goddess, shine upon thy land. Give it beauty and peace and joy." Then mother and son returned to the hut. Ayame plied her shuttle, and Umewaki left her to wander in the woods.

Noon came. " My boy has met some wood-cutter; he talks with him in the shade of the pine trees," she thought. As the evening drew on, she said, " He is with little Kime, his play-mate, but I shall soon hear his soft footstep." Night fell. " Once only has he been so late; when he went to Matsue with the good Shijo." She looked through the paper window, and then stepped out. The hills cast a mysterious shadow on the surface of the lake. Still there was no sign of Umewaki. The mother called his name. No response came save the echo of her own voice. Now she searched far and near. To every peasant she put the question, " Have you seen my Umewaki?" But she always received the same answer. At last she returned home weary: " He may be there waiting for me," she thought. It was midnight : the hut was empty. Ayame was heavy at heart, and as she lay upon her mat she wept bitterly, and cried to the gods to give her back her son. So the night passed. In the morning she learned that a band of robbers had been seen among the mountains.

Poor Umewaki had, in truth, been stolen by the robbers. He was watched night and day, and had no chance of escape. From town to town they travelled. Through strange villages where the name of Buddha was upon the lips of the people, across great plains un-sheltered by mountains. The summer passed, and autumn came. Still the men would not let Umewaki go. They treated him cruelly, and he began to pine away. Then the robbers knew that he was of no use to them. As they neared Yedo, they left him, faint and weary, on the roadside. A kind man of Mukochima found the poor little fellow and carried him to his home. But Umewaki had not long to live. On the fifteenth day of the third month, the day sacred to the awakening of the Spring, he opened his eyes, and called to the good

woman who tended him, " Tell my dear mother
that I love her, and would stay with her, but
the Lady of the Great Light calls me, and I
must obey."

Ayame had left her quiet hut by the lake of
Shinji to follow the men who had stolen her son.
The autumn and the winter had gone by, and
still she persevered. As she passed through
Mukochima, she heard that a poor boy was
dead, and soon found that it was her son.
She went to the house where he had been
cared for, and the woman gave her Umewaki's
message.

In the evening, when all was quiet, Ayame
crept to the graveside of her child. Near it a
sacred willow was planted. The slender tree
moved in the wind. There was a whispered
sound : the voice of Umewaki speaking softly
to the mother from his place of rest. She
was happy.

Every evening she came to listen to the
sighing of the willow. Every evening she lay
down happy to have spoken to her son.

On the fifteenth day of the third month,
the day of the awakening of the Spring, many

pilgrims visit the resting-place of Umewaki. If it rains on that day, the people say, " Umewaki weeps."

The willow is under the protection of the gods. Storm and rain can do it no hurt.

The Child of

the Forest

The Child of the Forest

SAKATO-NO-
TOKI-YUKI
was a brave warrior
at the court of Kyōto.
He fought for the Mina-
moto against the Taira, but
the Minamoto were defeated,
and Sakato's last days were spent as a
wandering exile. He died of a broken heart.
His widow, the daughter of a noble house,
escaped from Kyōto, and fled eastward to the
rugged Ashigara mountains. No one knew
of her hiding-place, and she had no enemies

to fear save the wild beasts who lived in the forest. At night she found shelter in a rocky cave.

A son was born to her whom she named Kintaro, the Golden Boy. He was a sturdy little fellow, with ruddy cheeks and merry laughing eyes. Even as he lay crowing in his bed among the fern, the birds that alighted on his shoulder peeped trustfully into his eyes, and he smiled. Thus early the child and the birds were comrades. The butterfly and the downy moth would settle upon his breast, and tread softly over his little brown body.

Kintaro was not as other children—there was something strange about him. When he fell, he would laugh cheerily ; if he wandered far into the wood, he could always find his way home ; and, when little more than a chubby babe, he could swing a heavy axe in circles round his head. In the remote hills he had no human companions, but the animals were his constant playfellows. He was gentle and kind-hearted, and would not willingly hurt any living creature ; therefore it was that the birds and all the forest people looked upon Kintaro as one of themselves.

Among Kintaro's truest friends were the bears who dwelt in the woods. A mother bear often carried him on her back to her home. The cubs ran out and greeted him joyfully, and they romped and played together for hours. They wrestled and strove in friendly rivalry. Sometimes Kintaro would clamber up the smooth-barked monkey tree, sit on the topmost branch, and laugh at the vain attempts of the shaggy little fellows to follow him. Then came supper-time and the feast of liquid honey.

But the Golden Boy loved best of all to fly through the air with his arms round the neck of a gentle-eyed stag. Soon after dawn, the deer came to awaken the sleeper, and, with a farewell kiss to his mother and a morning caress to the stag, Kintaro sprang on his back and was carried, with swift bounds, up mountain side, through valley and thicket, until the sun was high in the heavens. When they came to a leafy spot in the woods and heard the sound of falling water, the stag grazed among the high fern while Kintaro bathed in the foaming torrent.

Thus mother and son lived securely in their home among the mountains. They saw no human being save the few woodcutters who penetrated thus far into the forest, and these simple peasants did not guess their noble birth. The mother was known as Yama-uba-San, "The Wild Nurse of the Mountain," and her son as "Little Wonder."

Kintaro reigned as prince of the forest, beloved of every living creature. When he held his court, the bear and the wolf, the fox and the badger, the marten and the squirrel, and many other courtiers were seated around him. The birds, too, flocked at his call. The eagle and the hawk flew down from the distant heights; the crane and the heron swept over the plain, and feathered friends without number thronged the branches of the cedars. He listened as they told of their joys and their sorrows, and spoke graciously to all, for Kintaro had learned the language and lore of the beasts, and the birds, and the flowers, from the Tengus, the wood-elves.

Kintaro reigned as prince of the forest, beloved of every living creature.

"

The Tengus, who live in the rocky heights of the mountains and in the topmost branches of lofty trees, befriended Kintaro and became his teachers. As he was truthful and good, he had nothing to fear from them; but the Tengus are dreaded by deceitful boys, whose tongues they pull out by their roots and carry away.

These elves are strange beings: with the body of a man, the head of a hawk, long, long noses, and two powerful claws on their hairy hands and feet. They are hatched from eggs, and, in their youth, have feathers and wings: later, they moult and wear the garb of men. On their feet are stilt-like clogs about twelve inches high. They stalk proudly along with crossed arms, head thrown back, and long nose held high in the air; hence the proverb, "He has become a Tengu."

The headquarters of the tribe are in the Ōyama mountain, where lives the Dai-Tengu, their leader, whom all obey. He is even more proud and overbearing than his followers, and his nose is so long that one of his ministers always precedes him that it may not be injured. A long grey beard reaches to his girdle, and moustaches hang from his mouth to his chin. His sceptre is a fan of seven feathers, which he carries in his left hand. He rarely speaks, and is thus accounted wondrous wise. The Raven-Tengu is his chief minister; instead of a nose and mouth, he has a long beak. Over the left shoulder is slung an executioner's axe, and in his hand he bears the book of Tengu wisdom.

The Tengus are fond of games, and their long noses are useful in many ways. They serve as swords for fencing, and as poles on the point of which to balance bowls of water with gold-fish. Two noses joined together form a tight-rope on which a young Tengu, sheltered by a paper umbrella and leading a little dog, dances and jumps through hoops; the while an old Tengu sings a dance-tune and another beats time with a fan. Some among the older Tengus are very wise. The most famous of all is he who dwells on the Kurama mountain, but hardly less wise is the Tengu who undertook the education of

Kintaro. At nightfall he carried the boy to the nest in the high rocks. Here he was taught the wisdom of the elves, and the speech of all the forest tribes.

One day, Little Wonder was at play with some young Tengus, but they grew tired and flew up to their nest, leaving Kintaro alone. He was angry with them, and shook the tree with all his strength, so that the nest fell to the ground. The mother soon returned, and was in great distress at the loss of her children. Kintaro's kind heart was touched, and, with the little ones in his arms, he swarmed up the tree and asked pardon. Happily they were unhurt, and soon recovered from their fright. Kintaro helped to rebuild the nest, and brought presents to his playfellows.

Now it happened that, as the hero Raiko, who had fought so bravely against the *oni*, passed through the forest, he came upon Little Wonder wrestling with a powerful bear. An admiring circle of friends stood around. Raiko, as he looked, was amazed at the strength and courage of the boy. The combat over, he asked Kintaro his name and his story, but the child could only lead him to his mother. When she learned that the man before her was indeed Raiko, the mighty warrior, she told him of her flight from Kyōto, of the birth of Kintaro, and of their secluded life among the mountains. Raiko wished to take the boy away and train him in arms, but Kintaro loved the forest. When, however, his mother spoke, he was ready to obey. He called together his friends, the beasts and the birds, and, in words that are remembered to this day, bade them all farewell.

The mother would not follow her son to the land of men, but Kintaro, when he became a great hero, often came to see her in the home of his childhood.

The peasants of the Ashigara still tell of The Wild Nurse of the Mountains and Little Wonder.

The Vision of
Tsunu

The Vision of Tsunu

WHEN the
five tall
pine trees on the
windy heights of
Mionoseki were but tiny shoots, there lived in
the Kingdom of the Islands a pious man. His
home was in a remote hamlet surrounded by
mountains and great forests of pine. Tsunu
had a wife and sons and daughters. He
was a woodman, and his days were spent in

143

the forest and on the hillsides. In summer he was up at cock-crow, and worked patiently, in the soft light under the pines, until nightfall. Then, with his burden of logs and branches, he went slowly homeward. After the evening meal, he would tell some old story or legend. Tsunu was never weary of relating the wondrous tales of the Land of the Gods. Best of all he loved to speak of Fuji-yama, the mountain that stood so near his home.

In times gone by, there was no mountain where now the sacred peak reaches up to the sky; only a far-stretching plain bathed in sunlight all day. The peasants in the district were astonished, one morning, to behold a mighty hill where before had been the open plain. It had sprung up in a single night, while they slept. Flames and huge stones were hurled from its summit; the peasants feared that the demons from the under-world had come to wreak vengeance upon them. But for many generations there have been peace and silence on the heights. The good Sun-Goddess loves Fuji-yama. Every evening she lingers on his summit, and when at last she leaves him, his lofty crest is bathed in soft purple light. In the evening the Matchless Mountain seems to rise higher and higher into the skies, until no mortal can tell the place of his rest. Golden clouds enfold Fuji-yama in the early morning. Pilgrims come from far and near, to gain blessing and health for themselves and their families from the sacred mountain.

On the self-same night that Fuji-yama rose out of the earth, a strange thing happened in the mountainous district near Kyōto. The inhabitants were awakened by a terrible roar, which continued throughout the night. In the morning every mountain had disappeared; not one of the hills that they loved was to be seen. A blue lake lay before them. It was none other than the lute-shaped Lake Biwa. The mountains had, in truth, travelled under the earth for more than a hundred miles, and now form the sacred Fuji-yama.

As Tsunu stepped out of his hut in the morning, his eyes sought the Mountain of the Gods. He saw the golden clouds, and the beautiful story was in his mind as he went to his work.

One day the woodman wandered farther than usual into the forest. At noon he was in a very lonely spot. The air was soft and sweet, the sky so blue that he looked long at it, and then took a deep breath. Tsunu was happy.

Now his eye fell on a little fox who watched him curiously from the bushes. The creature ran away when it saw that the man's attention had been attracted. Tsunu thought, " I will follow the little fox and see where she goes." Off he started in pursuit. He soon came to a bamboo thicket. The smooth slender stems waved dreamily, the pale green leaves still sparkled with the morning dew. But it was not this which caused the woodman to stand spellbound. On a plot of mossy grass beyond the thicket, sat two maidens of surpassing beauty. They were partly shaded by the waving bamboos, but their faces were lit up by the sunlight. Not a word came from their lips, yet Tsunu knew that the voices of both must be sweet as the cooing of the wild dove.

On a plot of mossy grass beyond the thicket, sat two maidens of surpassing beauty.

The maidens were graceful as the slender willow, they were fair as the blossom of the cherry tree. Slowly they moved the chessmen which lay before them on the grass. Tsunu hardly dared to breathe, lest he should disturb them. The breeze caught their long hair, the sunlight played upon it. . . . The sun still shone. . . . The chess-men were still slowly moved to and fro. . . . The woodman gazed enraptured.

"But now," thought Tsunu, "I must return, and tell those at home of the beautiful maidens." Alas, his knees were stiff and weak. "Surely I have stood here for many hours," he said. He leaned for support upon his axe; it crumbled into dust. Looking down, he saw that a flowing white beard hung from his chin.

For many hours the poor woodman tried in vain to reach his home. Fatigued and wearied, he came at last to a hut. But all was changed. Strange faces peered curiously at him. The speech of the people was unfamiliar. "Where are my wife and my children?" he cried. But no one knew his name.

Finally, the poor woodman came to understand that seven generations had passed since he bade farewell to his dear ones in the early morning. While he had gazed at the beautiful maidens, his wife, his children, and his children's children, had lived and died.

The few remaining years of Tsunu's life were spent as a pious pilgrim to Fuji-yama, his well-loved mountain.

Since his death he has been honoured as a saint who brings prosperity to the people of his native country.

Princess Fire-Fly

D EEP in the pinky petals of a lotus bloom
that grew in the castle moats of Fukui,
in Echizen, lived Hi-O, the King of the Fire-
Flies. In this beautiful flower his daughter,
the Princess Hotaru, passed her childhood
exploring every shady nook and fragrant
corner of the bell-like palace, listening to the
buzz of life around, and peeping over the edge
of the petals at the wonderful world which

lay mysteriously beyond. Hotaru-Himé had few youthful companions, but, as she daily bade her father farewell, she dreamed of the time when she, too, would fly abroad, and her brilliant light would attract universal admiration.

Gradually, a beautiful sheen o'erspread her body; night by night it became brighter, until at last her home, in the hours of darkness, was as a globe of coral wherein shone a lamp of gold. So glorious was her light that the stars paled before it, and the bright sickle moon withdrew behind a cloud from jealousy.

Himé was now allowed to fly from her home, to loiter among the pleasant rice fields, and to explore the indigo meadows which lay far off on the horizon. She had no lack of friends and would-be lovers; thousands of insects, attracted by her magic light, came and offered their homage, but Himé never forgot that she was of royal blood, and, while she haughtily thanked her many suitors, none found a way into her heart.

But the Princess whispered to herself, "Only he who loves me more than
life shall call me bride."

One evening the Princess, seated on a throne formed by the heart of the lotus, held her court. Soon the faint roseate petals of the flower were thronged with a host of ardent lovers. But the Princess whispered to herself, "Only he who loves me more than life shall call me bride."

The golden beetle laid his fortunes at her feet, the cockchafer wooed her in passionate words, the dragon-fly proudly proffered his hand, and the hawk-moth humbly, yet persistently, addressed her. Countless other insects gained audience, but her answer was ever the same, "Go, and bring me fire, and I will be your bride."

One by one they took wing, enraptured by the hope of success, and unconscious that they were all bent on the selfsame errand. The hawk-moth entered the Buddhist Temple and circled round and round the tall wax lights, until, in an ecstasy of love, he flew into the flame, exclaiming, "Now to win the Princess or meet my death!" His poor singed body fell heavily to the ground. The beetle watched intently, for a moment or two, the log fire crackling on the hearth, and then, regardless of his fate, boldly caught at a tongue of flame he hoped to carry to Himé— but his end was that of the hawk-moth. The dragon-fly, notwithstanding his sunlit splendours, could not fulfil the bidding of the Lady of the Lotus Bloom; he also fell a prey to her imperious command. Other lovers there were who tried to steal from the diamond his heart of fire, who winged their way to the summit of Fukui, or sped to the depths of the valleys in search of the talisman that was to make Himé their bride. The sun rose in morning splendour over untold numbers of dead bodies, which alone remained to tell of the great devotion that had inspired the lovers of Princess Hotaru.

Now tidings came to Hi-Maro, a Prince of the Fire-Flies living hard by, that the Princess Hotaru was exceedingly beautiful; whereupon he flew swiftly to her home among the lotus flowers. Even as, with a flood of golden light, he entered, the charms of Himé were not dimmed. One look passed between the youth and the maiden, and then each felt that a great love filled their hearts. Hi-Maro wooed and wed, and for many years lived happily with Hotaru-Himé in the castle moats of Fukui.

Centuries have passed since Hi-Maro won his bride, and still the dazzling fire-fly Princesses send their insect lovers in search of fire.

The Sparrow's Wedding

The Sparrow's Wedding

IN the heart of a forest of pine-trees that lay in a remote corner of the Land of the Dragon-Fly, dwelt Chiyotaro, a prosperous sparrow, who was honoured and beloved alike by his family and friends. He had many beautiful children, but not one with manners more distinguished, or heart more true, than Tschiotaro. He was the life of the little household; merry as the summer-day is long, and talkative as only a sparrow can be.

Tschiotaro would fly afar through the woods, and across the surrounding plains; indeed, at times, he would even come within sight of the towering peaks of the Matchless Mountain. With the first whisper of the approach of sundown, he would wing his way homeward, to delight the loved ones in the pine forest with the story of his day's adventures. Laughter and sounds of glee echoed through the twilight, as the sparrow family listened to Tschiotaro's chatter. Then came the hush of night, and there was silence in the depths of the wood.

One sunny morning Tschiotaro chirped his farewell, and flew off he knew not whither. At last, he alighted in the shadowy bamboo grove where Kosuzumi, the tongue-cut sparrow, dwelt. Truly the gods had favoured him in guiding his flight to this spot. Kosuzumi was beautiful, but her daughter Osuzu was even more lovely. She was blithe, warm-hearted, and winsome;

simple, too, was the maiden whose days had been spent in the cool shade of the bamboo thicket. Tschiotaro had only to see her to love her. At first, it is true, he was a little shy, and hopped around the beautiful one with mute appeal in his tiny sparkling eyes ; but when he saw that Osuzu smiled and peeped coyly at him, he grew bolder, and even ventured to address her. Little by little the talk became more animated : reserve vanished, and mutual confidences passed. Tschiotaro and Osuzu had, in truth, entered the Garden of Bliss, which is known in the feathered world of Japan as *Okugi*. Time sped apace, and the hour of parting came all too quickly. Tschiotaro assured Osuzu that he would soon return. As he travelled through the summer air, laden with the fragrance of myriad flowers, a deep joy filled his heart and added zest to his flight. Osuzu, happy in her new-found love, was rocked peacefully to sleep by the swaying of the bamboo branches in the soft breeze.

Tschiotaro lost no time in making known

to his father his love for the beautiful daughter of Kosuzumi, and declared that she, and none other, should be his bride. The old one heard the news with surprise. Rich and respected as he was, he could not permit his son to marry the first maiden with whom he fell in love ; but as Chiyotaro sat contentedly in a quiet nook of his rustling home, his love for his son, and the desire to see him happy, outweighed all other considerations. He said, " If Osuzu be good and true, I will not refuse to give my consent." Even before he heard that Osuzu belonged to a family honoured far and wide, that her home was dainty, and that her mother was the famous tongue-cut sparrow, Chiyotaro had determined that nothing should cloud his son's happiness.

After the lapse of a day or two, Tschiotaro's glowing story was confirmed by the wise ones among the sparrows. Father and mother were content, and, according to old custom, an envoy was despatched to the parents of Osuzu with a formal offer of marriage. The family in the bamboo thicket, after due deliberation, consented to meet Chiyotaro. All went well. The wedding day was speedily fixed, and all manner of preparations were made for the auspicious event.

The home that was to shelter Tschiotaro and Osuzu was built with the greatest care in the upper branches of a beautiful cherry tree, whose pure white petals in blossom-time would lend fragrance and peace to the happy retreat. Many were the gifts which arrived to adorn, and add comfort to, the new abode. Sparrows from far and near vied with one another in the delicacy and variety of their offerings, until the dwelling was wondrously enticing.

Just before the wedding day, Osuzu rejoiced at the arrival of rare gifts from her beloved Tschiotaro. An *obi* of dewdrops, which held in them the secrets of the sun; a head-dress, fashioned of the slender petals of a mountain flower; and tiny moss sandals, so soft and exquisite that she donned them at once for very love and pride;

these and many other gifts did Tschiotaro bestow. Nor were Osuzu's parents unmindful of their duties. A grand robe of ceremony, woven of the pinky blossom of the peach, as well as *saké* and luscious fruit, were sent to Tschiotaro.

The morning of the marriage dawned. By the time the sun touched with glory the peak of Fusi-yama, the sparrow families were busy preparing for the day's festivities. Long ere the purple shadows had lifted from the valleys, the wedding procession had assembled from copse, and hedgerow, and woodland. Never before had such a concourse of sparrows been seen. Tschiotaro was widely beloved, and the beauty of Osuzu had become noised abroad.

On arrival at their new home, the bride and bridegroom sipped thrice of the three cups of rice wine which consecrated their union, and afterwards the whole company drank freely to the health and well-being of the newly wedded pair. Sounds of revelry and rejoicing lasted until the late evening; and long after the sun had bade his daily farewell to the cherry grove the sparrows still chattered and twittered.

As the moon, with her attendant maidens, rose slowly in the heavens, the festal sounds died away and silence reigned.

Tschiotaro and Osuzu spent many happy years of wedded sparrowhood. They had children fair and graceful as themselves, and never had cause to regret their loving union.

The Love of the

Snow - White Fox

The Love of the Snow-White Fox

IN Idzumo, the Province of the Gods, are many foxes. There the wicked Ninko, in league with the *oni*, prowls about at nightfall and carries away the souls of little children, he robs the poor man of his rice and millet, and bewitches the maidens who cross his path. There, too,

173

is his enemy the Inari fox, who is kind of heart. The Inari loves the children, and warns the anxious mothers when Ninko is near; he guards the store of the peasant, and comes to the aid of maidens in distress.

Many centuries ago, there lived a young Inari fox. She was snow-white, and her eyes were keen and intelligent. She was beloved by all the good people for miles around. They were glad if, in the evening, she knocked softly with her tail against the window of their hut; when she entered she would play with the children, eat of their humble fare, and then trot away. The god Inari protected those who were kind to her. The Ninko foxes hated her.

There were hunters in the country of Idzumo who thirsted for the blood of the beautiful white fox. Once or twice she nearly lost her life at the hands of these cruel men.

One summer afternoon, she was frisking about in the woods with some young fox friends, when two men caught sight of her. They were fleet of foot and had dogs by their side. Off ran the white fox. The men uttered an excited cry and gave chase. Instead of going towards the open plain, she made for the Temple of Inari Daim-yojin. "There surely I will find a safe refuge from my pursuers," she thought.

Now Yaschima, a young prince of the noble house of Abe, was in the temple, deep in meditation. The white fox, whose strength was almost spent, ran fearlessly up to him and took refuge beneath the thick folds of his robe. Yaschima was moved with pity, and did all in his power to soothe the poor frightened creature. He said, "I will protect you, little one; you have nothing to fear." The fox looked up at him, and seemed to understand. She ceased to tremble. Then the Prince went to the door of the great temple. Two men hastened up to him and asked if he had seen a pure white fox. "It must have run into the Temple of Inari. We would have its blood to cure the sickness of one of our family." But Yaschima, faithful to his promise, answered: "I have been in the temple praying to the good god, but I can tell you nothing of the fox." The men were about to leave him, when, behind his robe, they spied a white bushy tail. Fiercely they demanded that he should stand aside. The Prince firmly refused. But, intent on their prey, the men attacked him, and he was obliged to draw his sword in self-defence. At this moment Yaschima's father, a brave old man, came up; he rushed upon the enemies of his son, but a deadly blow, which Yaschima could not avert, struck him down. Then the young Prince was very wroth, and, with two mighty strokes, he felled his adversaries to the ground.

The loss of his beloved father filled Yaschima with grief. He did not break out into loud lamentation, for the sorrow lay too near his heart.

Then a sweet song fell on his ear. It came from the temple. As he re-entered the sacred building, a beautiful maiden stood before him. She turned, and saw that he was in deep trouble. The Prince told her of the snow-white fox, and the cruel hunters, and the death of his father whom he loved. The maiden spoke tender words of sympathy; her voice was so

With two mighty strokes, he felled his adversaries to the ground.

M

soft and sweet that the sound brought comfort to him. When Yaschima learned that the maiden was true, that her heart was as pure and beautiful as her face, he loved her, and asked her to be his bride. She replied, very gently, "I already love you. I know that you are good and brave, and I would solace you for the loss of your father."

They were wed. Yaschima did not forget the death of his father, but he remembered that his beautiful wife had then been given to him. For some time they lived happily together. The days passed swiftly. Yaschima ruled his people wisely, and his fair Princess was ever by his side. Each morning they went to the temple, and thanked the good god Inari for the joy that had come to them.

Now a son was born to the Prince and Princess. They gave him the name of Seimei. Thereafter the Princess became sorely troubled. She sat alone for hours, and tears sprang to her eyes when Yaschima asked her the cause of her sorrow. One day she took his hand and said, "Our life here has been very beautiful. I have given you a son to be with you always. The god Inari now tells me that I must leave you. He will guard you as you guarded me from the hunters at the door of the great temple. I am none other than the snow-white fox whose life you saved." Once more she looked into his eyes, and then, without a word, she was gone.

Yaschima and Seimei lived long in the Province of the Gods. They were greatly beloved, but the snow-white fox was seen no more.

Nedzumi

Nedzumi

IN the Central Land
of Reed-Plains
dwelt two rats. Their
home was in a lonely
farmstead surrounded by rice fields. Here
they lived happily for so many years that
the other rats in the district, who had
constantly to change their quarters, believed
that their neighbours were under the special
protection of Fukoruku Jin, one of the Seven

Gods of Happiness, and the Patron of Long Life.

These rats had a large family of children. Every summer day they led the little ones into the rice fields, where, under shelter of the waving stalks, the young rats learned the history and cunning of their people. When work was done, they would scamper away and play with their friends until it was time to return home.

The most beautiful of these children was Nedzumi, the pride of her parents' heart. She was truly a lovely little creature, with sleek silvery skin, bright intelligent eyes, tiny up-standing ears, and pearly white teeth. It seemed to the fond father and mother that no one was great enough to marry their daughter, but, after much pondering, they decided that the most powerful being in the whole universe should be their son-in-law.

The parents discussed the weighty question with a trusted neighbour, who said, "If you would wed your daughter to the most powerful being in the universe, you must ask the sun to marry her, for his empire knows no bounds."

How they mounted through the skies, no rat can tell. The sun gave them audience and listened graciously as they said, "We would give you our daughter to wife." He smiled and rejoined, "Your daughter is indeed beautiful, and I thank you for coming so far to offer her to me. But, tell me, why have you chosen me out of all the ,world?" The rats made answer, "We would marry our Nedzumi to the mightiest being, and you alone wield world-wide sway." Then the sun replied, "Truly my kingdom is vast, but oftentimes, when I would illumine the world, a cloud floats by and covers me. I cannot pierce the cloud; therefore you must go to him if your wish is to be attained."

In no way discouraged, the rats left the sun and came to a cloud as he rested after a flight through the air. The cloud received them less cordially than the sun, and replied to their offer, with a look of mischief in his dusky eyes, "You are mistaken if you think that I am the most powerful being. It is true that I sometimes hide the sun, but I cannot withstand the force of the wind. When he begins to blow

I am driven away, and torn in pieces. My strength is not equal to the power of the wind."

A little saddened, the rats, intent on their daughter's future prosperity, waylaid the wind as he swept through a pine forest. He was about to awaken the plain beyond, to stir the grass and the flowers into motion. The two anxious parents made known their mission. This was the whispered reply of the wind: "It is true that I have strength to drive away the clouds, but I am powerless against the wall which men build to keep me back. You must go to him if you would have the mightiest being in the world for your son-in-law. Indeed I am not so mighty as the wall."

The rats, still persistent in their quest, came to the wall and told their story. The wall answered, "True, I can withstand the wind, but the rat undermines me and makes holes through my very heart. To him you must go if you would wed your daughter to the most powerful being in the world. I cannot overcome the rat."

NEDZUMI

And now the parent rats returned to their
home in the farmstead. Nedzumi, their beautiful daughter with the silken coat and sparkling
eyes, rejoiced when she heard that she was to
marry one of her own people, for her heart
had already been given to a playfellow of the
rice fields. They were married, and lived for
many years as king and queen of the rat
world.

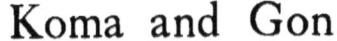

Koma and Gon

Koma and Gon

MANY moons ago, a teacher of music
lived not far from Kyoto. A faithful
serving-woman and a beautiful cat were his
sole companions. Gon was a handsome fellow,
with sleek coat, bushy tail, and grass-green
eyes that glowed in the darkness. His master
loved him, and would say as the cat purred
by his side in the evening, "Nothing shall
part us, old friend."

O-Ume was a happy maiden whose home lay in the midst of the plum groves. Her chief pet was a little cat. Koma had very winning ways; her mistress delighted to watch her. She blinked so prettily, she ate so daintily, she licked her rose-red nose so carefully with her tiny tongue, that O-Ume would catch her up, and say fondly, " Koma, Koma, you are a good cat. I am sure your ancestors shed tears when our Lord Buddha died. You shall never leave me."

It happened that Gon and Koma met, and fell deeply in love with one another. Gon was so handsome that any of the cats in the district would gladly have been his mate, but he did not deign to notice one of them. When he saw the little maid Koma, his heart beat quickly.

The cats were in great distress, for neither the music-master nor O-Ume would hear of parting with their pet. Gon's master would willingly have taken Koma to live with him, but O-Ume would not hear of this ; nor were Koma's entreaties more successful.

It was the seventh night of the seventh

moon, the night sacred to lovers in the Land
of Great Peace, when Kingen crosses the
Silver River of Heaven and Shakujo joyfully
embraces him. Gon and Koma left their
homes and fled together. It was a moonbright night, and the cats were light of heart
as they scampered through the fields of rice
and across the great open plains. When day
broke, they were near a palace which stood in
a large park, full of stately old trees and ponds
covered with sweet lotus-blooms. Koma said,
"If only we could live in that palace, how
glorious it would be!" As she spoke, a fierce
dog caught sight of the cats, and bounded towards them angrily. Koma gave a cry of
terror, and sprang up a cherry tree. Gon did
not stir. "Dear Koma shall see that I am a
hero, and would rather lose my life than run
away." But the dog was powerful, and would
have killed Gon. He was almost upon the
brave cat, when a serving-man drove him off,
and carried Gon into the palace. Poor little
Koma was left alone to lament her loss.

The Princess who lived in the palace was
overjoyed when Gon was brought to her.

Many days passed before he was allowed out
of her sight. Then he hunted far and near for
his fair lover, but all in vain. "My Koma is
lost to me for ever," he sighed.

Now the Princess lived in splendour and
happiness. She had but one trouble; a great
snake loved her. At all hours of the day and
night the animal would creep up and try to
come near her. A constant guard was kept,
but still the serpent, at times, succeeded in
gaining the door of her chamber. One afternoon, the Princess was playing softly to herself
on the *koto*, when the snake crept unobserved
past the guards and entered her room. In a
moment, Gon sprang upon its neck and bit it
so furiously that the hideous creature soon lay
dead. The Princess heard the noise and
looked round. When she saw that Gon had
risked his life for her, she was deeply moved;
she stroked him and whispered kind words
into his ear. He was praised by the whole
household, and fed upon the daintiest morsels
in the palace. But there was a cloud upon his
happiness: the loss of Koma.

On a summer day he lay sunning himself

before the door of the palace. Half asleep, he looked out upon the world and dreamed of the moonlight night when he and Koma escaped from their former homes. In the park a big cat was ill-treating a little one, too fragile to take care of herself. Gon jumped up and flew to her aid. He soon drove the cruel cat away; then he turned towards the little one to ask if she were hurt Koma, his long-lost love, stood before him! Not the sleek, beautiful Koma of other days, for she was thin and sad, but her eyes sparkled when she saw that Gon was her deliverer.

The two cats went to the Princess. They told her the story of their love, their flight, their separation, and their reunion. She entered whole-heartedly into their new-found joy.

On the seventh night of the seventh moon Gon and Koma were married. The Princess watched over them, and they were happy. Many years passed. One day she found them curled up together. The two faithful hearts had ceased to beat.

www.ingramcontent.com/pod-product-compliance
Lightning Source LLC
Chambersburg PA
CBHW031956170626
46807CB00006B/2510